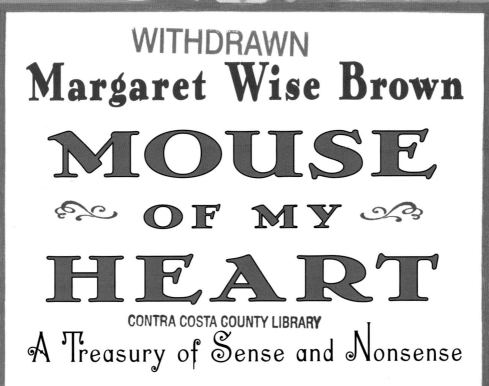

Margaret Wise Brown

MOUSE

OF MY

HEART

A Treasury of Sense and Nonsense

ILLUSTRATED BY

Loretta Krupinski

INTRODUCTION BY LEONARD S. MARCUS

HYPERION BOOKS FOR CHILDREN

NEW YORK

LIBRARY OF CONGRESS CATALOGING-IN-PUBLICATION DATA
Brown, Margaret Wise, 1910–1952.
Mouse of my heart : a treasury of sense and nonsense / Margaret Wise Brown;
illustrated by Loretta Krupinski.
p. cm.
Summary: A collection of stories and poems, arranged in the categories "Adventure,"
"Big and Little," "Bravery," "Love and Friendship," "Bedtime," "Happiness," "Belonging,"
"For a Rainy Day," "Nonsense," "Colors," and "Nature."
ISBN 0-7868-0628-1 (tr) — ISBN 0-7868-2546-4 (lib)
1. Children's literature, American. [1. Literature—Collections.]
I. Krupinski, Loretta, ill.   II. Title.
PZ7.B8163 Mo 2001   99-87878

Photo on page 1 by Consuelo Kanaga (1894–1978). The Brooklyn Museum
Gift of the Estate of Consuelo Kanaga through the Lerner Heller Gallery.

Contents

Margaret Wise Brown—Poet and Pioneer *by Leonard S. Marcus* / *1*

Adventure

A Cottontail Rabbit in a Cotton Field / *6*

Run, Bun, Run / *8*

Three White Rabbits Running / *9*

The Glorious Flight of the Mouse / *10*

The Little Pig's Picnic / *15*

Four Fur Feet / *25*

From a Hornet's Nest / *27*

Animals in the Snow / *28*

"Spring!" Sang the Bird / *39*

The Diggers / *40*

Big and Little

You Be Little and I'll Be Big / *48*

Baby Hippopotamus / *53*

Song of Little Things / *54*

A Bug's Poem / *55*

Said a Bug / *56*

The Three Snowmen / *59*

All the Little Fathers / *61*

What a Little Man / *64*

Contents

Bravery

The Flying Mouse / *72*

One Eye Open / *78*

The Tiger's Child / *80*

Brave Little Airplane / *81*

Love and Friendship

Mouse of My Heart / *84*

Little Brown Bird / *86*

The Lonely Little Colt / *87*

A Little Black Dog / *94*

Bedtime

Two Little Raccoons / *96*

Drowsy Little Bumblebee / *97*

When I Close My Eyes at Night / *98*

The Sleepy Bears / *99*

Under the Sun and the Moon / *102*

The Farmer's Lullaby / *106*

Happiness

The Barnyard Song / *108*

Where Is the Spring? / *110*

Red Cherries / *111*

O Pussywillows / *112*

Spring Still Spring / *114*

Contents

Belonging

I Dreamed of a Horse / 116
Three Baby Kittens / 117
The Ugly Duckling / 126
The Grasshopper and the Ants / 138

For a Rainy Day

The Hollow Tree / 148
Raindrops on the Willow Tree / 149
Smoky Nights / 150
Quiet Rain / 151
The Old Mill / 152

Nonsense

Nonsense Song / 162
Whoopsie Daisy! / 164
Snowballs and Sunshine / 165

Colors

Apple Trees / 172
Golden Air / 173
All the Bright Colors / 174

Nature

One Night / 176
The Life of a Leaf / 178
Dream of a Weed / 179
Clouds / 180

Index / 181

MOUSE
OF MY
HEART

Margaret Wise Brown

POET AND PIONEER

THE WINKING WIT AND POIGNANT LYRICISM of Margaret Wise Brown's poems and stories for children have touched and delighted generations. By now, most everyone with a small child finds their way to the great green room of *Goodnight Moon* and perhaps to one or more of the author's other well-known picture-book classics. Less well known is the fact that Brown (1910–1952) was a hugely prolific writer during her brief but brilliant career, which spanned the last years of the Great Depression and the first years of postwar baby-boom prosperity. In the pages that follow, readers have the chance to range widely in this beguiling author's less familiar and previously unpublished work. A rewarding experience awaits.

What is it about Margaret Wise Brown's words that has made them last? For one thing, Brown had an unerring grasp of the child's emotional point of view.

She knew that children feel lonely, neglected, angry, and sad, and that the young draw comfort from stories that show they are not alone in harboring such feelings. The author of *The Runaway Bunny* chose rabbits, piglets, kittens, and mice for subjects not only because small creatures make endearing characters but because in real life they, like children, must so often defend against their vulnerabilities.

1

Though small in stature, Brown's heroes never want for dignity or determination. The doughty piglet of "The Little Pig's Picnic" continues to search for her supper, no matter that one looming barnyard animal after another tries to shove her aside. Left alone in a meadow, the spindly-legged protagonist of "The Lonely Little Colt" soldiers on until he finds the friend he needs. It is hardly surprising that, of all fairy tales, Brown chose to retell Hans Christian Andersen's "The Ugly Duckling," one of children's literature's classic explorations of the theme of the little fellow compelled, through no fault of his own, to endure the towering indifference of others.

In each of these stories, Brown shines a sympathetic light on the difficulties children face daily. Equally compelling for her as material was the young child's sense of wonder at the world. For Brown, the challenge of writing for children consisted in large part of being imaginatively quick enough to capture in words that magical sense of the newness and wonder of everything. It is always fascinating to watch her take up the challenge, as she does, for instance, in the short verses "A Bug's Poem" and "Raindrops on the Willow Tree" and in the fantasy "Three Baby Kittens." Brown wrote like a painter, in arresting images and descriptive phrases of uncanny precision. A hawk goes "for a drift in the air;" bats "flutter . . . forth . . . like ragged scattered leaves." Words as finely tuned as these have the power to lift us out of ourselves. For Brown, the smallest detail—in or out of the great green room—always repays our close attention.

Yet the world revealed in her stories and poems is not only snug and secure but also a place of vast and wide-ranging possibilities. "The Old Mill" dramatizes the awesome power of nature as a storm bears down on an abandoned windmill and its animal inhabitants. The jaunty hero of "Four Fur Feet" goes out for a walk and blithely circles the globe. As much as anything, it is the untamed bigness of Brown's vision that sets her unsentimental writings apart from the usual run of literature for young children.

Brown herself hardly conformed to the sentimental stereotype of the spinsterly juveniles author. She had film-star good looks and lived fast and extravagantly, dividing her time between the social whirl of New York and the wild splendor of her island aerie off the coast of Maine. Although never a good student, she read widely and grew up with dreams of writing one day. It was while enrolled, so improbably for her, as a teacher trainee at New York's Bank Street College of Education, that she first considered writing for children. Almost from the start she found that picture-book writing came naturally to her, though as she later remarked: "We speak naturally and spend our whole lives trying to write naturally." During the next fifteen years, when she wrote more or less constantly, Brown became a consummate craftsman. One reason that her work continues to be read is that she so often achieved the kind of hard-won simplicity that comes of paring down one's thoughts and perceptions to their clearest possible form.

Like her heroes-in-letters Gertrude Stein and Virginia Woolf, Brown prided herself on being an experimental writer. Experimentation for her, however, was less a matter of art for art's sake than it was an effort to discover new ways of writing for children that matched their unfolding levels of awareness. With young children in mind, she devised simple rhyme schemes and easy-to-grasp word patterns, using these as building blocks for constructing a poem or tale. Consider, for instance, the opening lines of "All the Little Fathers":

> All the little fathers were chirping to their children.
> > Bird fathers!
> All the little fathers were giving their children bones to chew.
> > Dog fathers!
> All the little fathers were purring to their children.
> > Cat fathers! . . .

The poem follows the same clear pattern for several more stanzas; even a small child can quickly limn its design. Brown hoped that children would take up her simple patterns as jumping-off points for their own imaginings. Of all the creative impulses that define Margaret Wise Brown's unique contribution to children's literature, this, perhaps, was the most inspired one of all: her continual search for ways to involve children as collaborators. Long before "interactivity" had become a buzzword, Brown wrote open-ended stories and poems that let children have the last word.

—Leonard S. Marcus
New York
March 2000

Adventure

A Cottontail Rabbit in a Cotton Field

A cottontail rabbit in a cotton field

Jumped in the air and gave a squeal

His little tail flashed

White in the light

A cottontail flashing

In clear plain sight

But no one saw him in the cotton field

And only the cold wind heard him squeal.

Run, Bun, Run

Said a bun
To a bun,
"Why don't you run
Out in the grass
And have some fun?"

Said a bun
To a bun,
"I refuse to run
When I can sit
And dream in the sun."

Run, bun, run,
Or sit in the sun,
Sit in the sun,
Or run, bun, run.

Three White Rabbits Running

There were three white rabbits running

There were three white rabbits running

There were three white rabbits running

And they ran far away

And they ran far away

And they ran far away

Little tracks across the white snow

Rabbit tracks across the soft snow

Little tracks across the white snow

And they ran far away

And they ran far away

And they ran far away.

The Glorious Flight of the Mouse

A mouse too little to leave his hole

Said to his mother,

"Do you think me a mole?"

And he rolled his eyes and strolled out of the hole.

Up through a tunnel and out of the ground

And there in the green grass looked around

At a green grass forest everywhere

And above a sea of endless air—
About so much air he had never been told
When he breathed the air in his dark little hole.

He caught his breath,
He was scared to death
At so much air
Everywhere.

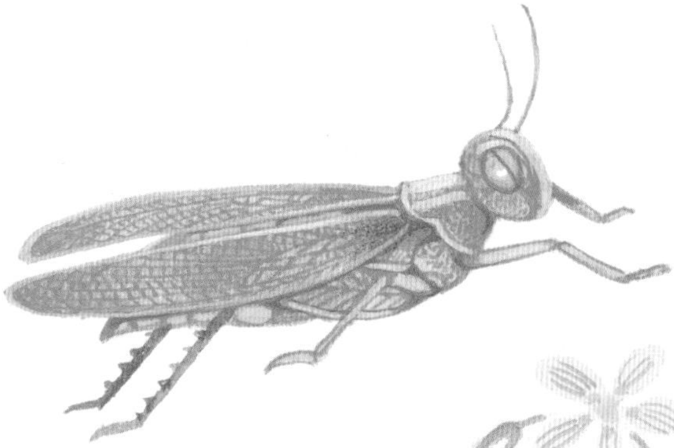

Then grasshopper, who was going somewhere,
Hopped out of the grass and into the air
But he didn't stay there,

So the little mouse said,

"Do you think you can scare

A little mouse with so much air?"

And he ran everywhere in the bright green grass.

Dandelions were yellow

Ladybugs red

And a pear blossom

Fell

On top of his head.

A violet bloomed right in his face

And a snail dashed by at a snail-like pace

And the mouse was so happy

There in the grass.

Until alas!

A hawk who had gone for a drift in the air

Spied the little mouse all furry down there

In the bright green grass.

And alas!

The next thing the mouse knew he was up in the air

Below was the green land everywhere,

White were the blossoms of the pear

But he couldn't see, so high was his head,

That dandelions were yellow and

Ladybugs red.

Then the hawk, spying another hawk,

Loosened his claws as he gave a squawk

    And the mouse dropped out

    Of the claws of the hawk

And fell to the ground

To continue his walk

And there in the green grass looked around

At a green grass forest everywhere

And above a sea of endless air.

The Little Pig's Picnic

NCE UPON A TIME in a barnyard there was a tiny little pig. There were eight little pigs and two big pigs, and there was a tiny little pig. Her name was Squeaker.

Squeaker was a runt pig, a very little pig. But her appetite was big.

It was as big as the appetite of a big pig. But poor little Squeaker, she did not get much to eat.

Every time old lady pig rolled over on her side to feed her little pigs, Squeaker would get pushed away. Squeaker would push and nudge, but the other little pigs would not budge. Not for such a little runt. Not for Squeaker!

"Oink! Oink!" Squeaker jumped up and down on the outside.

"No room! No room!" squeaked the little pigs. And

poor little Squeaker was left out in the cold. She could not get anything to eat.

So off went Squeaker, all through the wide barnyard, to look for her supper.

First she came to the pond where the swans were feeding. She sat down on her little pig seat on the bank and watched them. The swans floated over the water. Then quickly their heads darted down the full length of their necks into the water. They seemed to be eating something.

"Oink! Oink!" said Squeaker. "There must be something good down there. Nothing is too good for this little pig!"

So down Squeaker splashed into the water after a swan supper.

But a pig is not a swan. And Squeaker could not swim. Just in time to save her from drowning, the old mud turtle rose from the bottom of the pond like an island underneath her. And Squeaker rested on his shell.

"Little pig, little pig," said the old mud turtle, "go back and find a little pig's supper. This is no place for you. Get away from this pond and go find a pig's supper!"

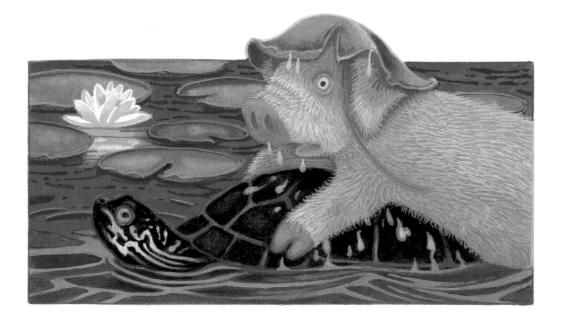

So, with a wiggle and a shake, off went little Squeaker again. Off she went to hunt for her supper.

She looked at the geese by the pond.

She looked in the fields at the grazing sheep.

Then, she looked in the barn and saw old Bossy Cow.

Old Bossy Cow was feeding her little bull calf. There must be something good in there for a little pig's supper. So Squeaker jumped up and down underneath old Bossy Cow.

"Oink! Oink!" said Squeaker. "Nothing's too good for this little pig!

"By the two little holes
In my little pig nose,
Milk would be good
For this little pig!"

But squeal and jump as she would, the milk was too far away. And the little calf mooed right in her face.

"Little pig, little pig," said old Bossy Cow. "Go and find a little pig's supper. You will never be able to reach as high as a calf!"

"Oink, oink, oink," sighed Squeaker and trotted out of the barn. She was so hungry!

And off she went, all through the wide barnyard, to look for her supper.

Just then Squeaker heard a man's voice calling, "Here, piggy, piggy, piggy!"

And Squeaker thought:

By the two little holes
In my little pig nose,
That must mean
A little pig's supper!

And she ran and she ran till she came to the trough where the hogs were eating. The mother pig was there, too, and the little pigs were all there with her.

Squeaker ran right over the backs of the baby pigs. She jumped up on the edge of the trough.

But an old hog said, "Ugh! Ugh! There's no room here for a baby pig. No room! No room!"

And Squeaker was rooted right out of there and sent squealing across the yard.

Then down by the chicken house she saw a big red dish of yellow cornmeal. "Oink!" said Squeaker. "That looks good to this little pig.

"By the two little holes
In my little pig nose,
There's a cornmeal supper
For this little pig!"

She ran right over to the pan and stuck her little pig nose in the cornmeal. She knocked all the little feathery chickens away. Such a noise they made! "Peep! Peep! Peep!"

The old mother hen came running with her beak wide open.

"Cluck-cluck! Ker-chuck!"

Squeaker didn't wait any longer. She started running away.

She knew there was no room in the chicken yard for this little pig.

Squeaker ran and ran all through the barnyard.

She watched the horses eat grass.

She watched the birds eat seeds.

She watched the donkey eat hay.

She watched the rooster eat worms.

But there was no supper for a little pig.

Poor little Squeaker! She ran all through the wide barnyard until she bumped into the corncrib. Bang! She knocked away the stick that held the door shut.

Down fell the corn! Down fell the golden ears of corn all over Squeaker. They tumbled in a golden pile around her. This was the little pig's picnic.

Then all the little chickens came running to the little pig's picnic.

The donkey brayed,
The rooster crowed,
The little colt neighed,
The little calf mooed,

And the oxen lowed
For the little pig's picnic!

And Squeaker ate and ate and ate and ate, there in the middle of the corn.

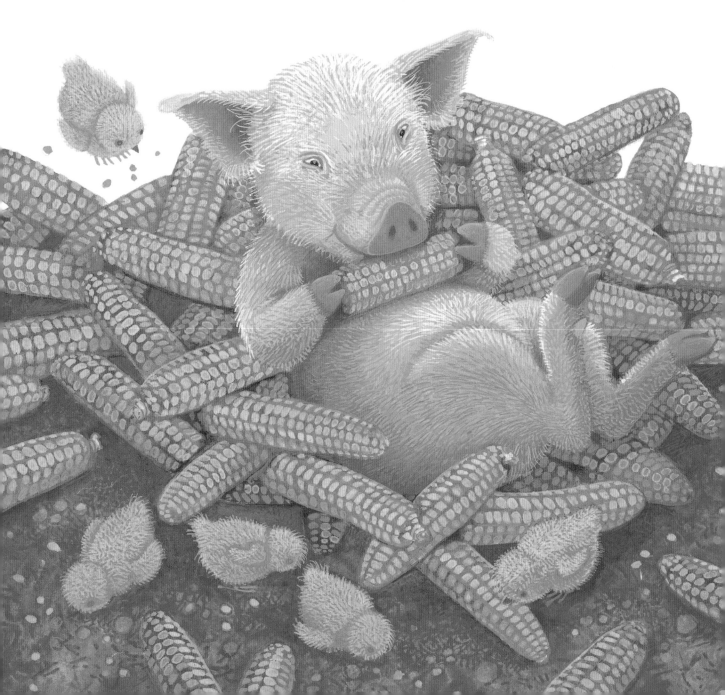

Four Fur Feet

Oh, he walked around the world on
    his four fur feet . . .
Oh, he walked around the world
On his four fur feet, his four fur feet,
    his four fur feet.
And he walked around the world on his four fur feet
And never made a sound—O.

Oh, he walked along the river on his four fur feet,
His four fur feet, his four fur feet.
He walked along the river on his four fur feet
And heard the boats go toot—O.

Then he walked by the railroad on his four fur feet
His four fur feet, his four fur feet.

He walked by the railroad
   on his four fur feet
And heard the trains go whoo—O.

Then he walked into the country on his four fur feet,
His four fur feet, four fur feet.
He walked into the country
   on his four fur feet
And heard the cows go moo—O.

Then he waded down a stream on his four fur feet,
His four fur feet, his four fur feet.
He waded down a stream on his four fur feet
And the water was all wet—O.

So, he folded up his four fur feet,
His four fur feet, his four fur feet.
So he folded up his four fur feet
And lay down in the grass—O.

From a Hornet's Nest

A swarm of hornets flew out from a hornet's nest
All on a summer's day.
Who to sting? Who to bite?
They buzzed and they buzzed and swarmed away
High in the sky where it was easy to fly
And look about with their hornet's eye
For anything for a hornet to sting
On foot or fin or feet or wing.
But this day they didn't see a thing
In wood or pond, in field or hay,
So they stung each other
And home they flew
All on a summer's day.

Animals in the Snow

The squirrel was cold.   The bird was cold.

The bunny was cold.

The cat was cold.   The dog was cold.

The day was cold.

SNOW!

Snow fell on the squirrel.

Snow fell on the bird.

Snow fell on the bunny.

Snow fell on the cat.

Snow fell on the dog.

It was snowing.

It snowed and snowed.

The squirrel ran home.

The bunny ran home.

The bird flew home.

The cat and the dog ran home.

And the snow was snowing,

Snowing and snowing.

The sun shone
on the squirrel's home.

The sun shone
on the bird's home.

The sun shone on
the bunny's home.

The sun shone
on the cat's home.

The sun shone
on the dog's home.

Then the sun came out and
shone on the snow.

30

The sun shone and shone.

And the squirrel came out of the squirrel's house.

And the bunny came out of the bunny's house.

And the bird came out of the bird's house.

And the dog came out of the dog's house.

And the cat came out of the cat's house.

And the squirrel and the bunny and the bird

And the dog and the cat sat in the sun.

A boy came out of the boy's house.

A girl came out of the girl's house.

And they sat in the sun.

Then they made tracks in the snow.

They made boy tracks and girl tracks.

And they saw squirrel tracks in the snow.

They saw bird tracks in the snow

And bunny tracks in the snow.

They saw cat tracks in the snow.

And dog tracks in the snow.

Then they made a snowman.

Then they made a snow dog

And a snow squirrel.

They made a snow bunny

And a snow bird

And a snow cat.

And the sun shone on the snow.

It shone and it shone and it shone.

Then the boy and the girl ran home.

And the next day when they came out

There was the sun.

But the snow had gone.

The snow dog and the snow cat

And the snow bird and the snow bunny

And the snow squirrel had gone.

The snowman was a puddle.

The snow bird was a puddle.

The snow dog was a puddle.

The snow cat was a puddle.

The snow squirrel was a puddle.

The snow bunny was a puddle.

But then they saw a real bird

And a real dog

And a real cat

And a real squirrel

And a real bunny.

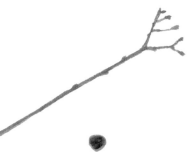

And the real dog

And the real cat

And the real squirrel

And the real bunny
ran into the woods.

And the real bird

And the boy and the girl
ran into the woods.

And in the woods the bird

    began to sing.

And the bunny and the dog ran.

And the squirrel and the cat

    ran up a tree.

And the puddles ran away.

And the sun shone and shone.

And they saw it—

They saw a snowdrop!

It was spring!

"Spring!" Sang the Bird

"Spring!" sang the bird.

"Spring! Spring! Spring!

The snow is gone.

The cold is gone.

Puddle, puddle, puddle,

The snow is gone.

The snowdrop's up,

And a bird can sing."

The Diggers

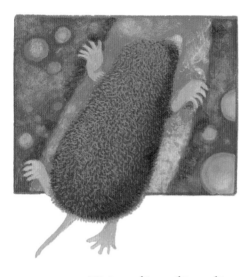

Dig dig dig
A mole was digging a hole.
Dig dig dig dig
A dog was digging a hole
Under a stone
To bury a bone.

Dig dig dig dig
A worm was digging a hole.
He swallowed the ground
As he wiggled around
And ate his way toward home.

Dig dig dig dig
A rabbit was digging a hole
Next to a mouse
Who was digging a house
In a little warm hole in the ground.

Dig dig dig dig
A pirate was digging a hole,
A hole in the sand to bury
  his gold
And the diamonds and rubies
  he stole.

Dig dig dig dig
In the city
A man was digging a hole.
Monday he dug,
And Tuesday he dug,
Wednesday, Thursday,
And Friday he dug,
And Saturday he dug until
He said, "I feel like a mouse
  or a mole.
This hole is too little.

41

This hole must get bigger,

As big as a giant could dig

If he were a digger."

And then came the big digger

Made by a man

To dig deeper and deeper—

To crunch up stones

And dinosaur bones

And cavemen's homes

And buried gnomes.

Dig dig dig dig

Down the dead-end street

The steam shovel dug its way.

Day after day after day after day,

It dug

Until the whole city street was dug away.

Its great jaws crunched full of dirt and rocks.

Its great arm lifted, paused, and swung

The world it had dug up

And put it somewhere else in the world.

And a great big hole ran under the city

And under a river

And into bright green country.

A man put a train in the hole,

And the train ran through the hole,

Under the street, under the city,

Under the river until it popped out of

the hole into the bright green country.

It went past ducks and geese

And donkeys and cows

And sheep and fields of galloping horses

Until it came to a mountain

And couldn't get through

And couldn't get over and

Couldn't get around, so it had to stop.

But not forever—

For down the track came another train

With another man

And tanks of oil

And gasoline.

And there on the last car

Rode the great digger, the steam shovel.

Under the mountain it dug away

Day after day after day after day

Until with one last bite it came to daylight

On the other side of the mountain.

And soon the train came through the mountain

And onto the great green plain.

And on went the train,

On and on down its long steel track,

And the smoke trailed back.

"That was easy," said the steam shovel.

"I'll dig a hole to China someday."

Big and Little

You Be Little and I'll Be Big

"'M SO LITTLE," said the bunny to the mouse, "and you're so big. Don't hurt me."

Now this morning the bunny felt very little inside, and so he was little. And it so happened that the mouse felt enormous inside that morning. Brave as a lion, fierce as a tiger, and big as an elephant. The sunflower seeds he had eaten the day before had agreed with him. He felt fine.

"All right," said the mouse, "I'll take care of you. Take a nap. You are so little you must sleep if your ears are to grow."

So the bunny curled himself up very little for a bunny and the mouse gave him just one sunflower seed—because he was so little.

When he woke up he felt much bigger.

So he went hopping through the woods to see his grandmother.

Now, the bunny's grandmother felt very little that day. Old rabbit ladies sometimes do feel very little. So the bunny took care of her all day long.

He rocked her in her rocking chair and he held her paw when the wind blew. Because the bunny's grandmother felt so little she was afraid of the sound of the wind in the trees.

And the bunny sang her a song.

"Big old Gran, big old Gran
How little you are
Like a grain of sand."

He sang his song to his little old Gran. And then he fed her a carrot. The bunny ate some, too.

"Now," said the bunny, "I feel little." After the carrot his grandmother felt very big again. So she picked the little bunny up in her lap and she rocked him to sleep, and she sang him a song.

"Little old Bun
Little old Bun,
How big are you?"

"Big as a goose,"
sang the little old Bun.
"Little old Gran,
How big are you?"

"Big as the land,"
sang his little old Gran.
"How big are you?"

But the bunny was so little he had fallen asleep, so his grandmother just hummed to him and rocked away.

Baby Hippopotamus

A baby hippopotamus looks

like a baby pig

Until a baby hippopotamus

grows up big

And then like a whale with a little short tail

He stays under the water and

swims like a whale.

Then comes out of the water

like a fat old pig

And wallows around when he grows big

Big as a hippopotamus.

Song of Little Things

Oh sing a song of little things
Of bugs and flies and
flickering wings

Of flakes of snow and drops of rain

And yellow flowers
in the lane

Of little pairs of squeaky shoes

And mice that laugh
until they snooze

Of stars and pins and crumbs of cake

And bugs that laugh themselves awake.

A Bug's Poem

Grass is green

And tall and high

And I am a bug

Looking up grass blades

Toward the sky

A striped sky

Striped with grass

Where green-striped

Grass-striped

White clouds

Pass

Beyond the high long

Straight green grass.

Said a Bug

Said a bug to a bug,
"Look away up high
At those great green grass blades
Piercing the sky."

Said a bug to a bug,
"How high is the sky
Above the grass blades,
Grass blades so high?"

Said the other bug,
"It depends on the eye
Of the bug that is looking
Up in the sky.
Some bugs crawl
And some bugs fly."

Said a bug to a bug,
"Buzz up and fly
Above those grass blades
Into the sky.
But don't bump
Into a butterfly!"

The Three Snowmen

Three snowmen tried to answer a question.

They couldn't agree.

The question was

WHAT MAKES A SNOWMAN DISAPPEAR?

"The wind," said the first snowman.

"The sun," said the second snowman.

"The rain," said the third snowman.

Then one day it was spring.

The wind blew,

The sun shone,

And the rain fell.

All in one day.

And all that was left of the snowmen was

Three puddles

Three pipes

Three sticks

Three silk hats

Six lump-of-coal eyes

And nine cocklebur buttons.

They had all been right.

All the Little Fathers

All the little fathers were chirping
to their children.
Bird fathers!

All the little fathers were giving their
children bones to chew.
Dog fathers!

All the little fathers were
purring to their children.
Cat fathers!

All the little fathers were hanging
by their tails.
Monkey fathers!

All the little fathers were
playing with their children.
Lion fathers!

All the little fathers were trying
to catch their children.
Panda fathers!

62

All the little fathers were
   hiding nuts with their children.
Squirrel fathers!

All the little fathers were showing
   their children how to run.
Rabbit fathers!

All the little fathers were putting
   their children to bed.
Fathers!

What a Little Man

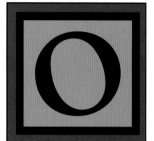

O NCE THERE WAS A LITTLE DOG who had never seen a child. One day he saw a little boy. He was so surprised he barked.

"What a little tiny man," said the dog.

"I'm not a little tiny man," said the child. "I am a little boy."

"What is the difference?" asked the dog.

"Ask any man," said the little boy.

So the dog walked along until he met a man.

"What is the difference between a man and a little boy?" asked the dog.

"One is little and one is big," said the man.

So the little dog wagged his tail and ran along.

Until suddenly he met a little girl. He was so surprised that he barked.

"What a tiny little woman," said the dog.

"I'm not a tiny little woman," said the little girl. "I am a little girl."

"What is the difference?" asked the dog.

"Ask any woman," said the little girl.

So the little dog walked along until he met a great big woman.

"What is the difference between a woman and a little girl?" asked the dog.

"One is little and one is big," said the woman, and she walked along.

So the little dog shook his head and ran off across the fields till he came to a stream, and there by the stream he saw a tiny little rabbit eating parsley.

"What a tiny little rabbit," said the dog.

"I am not a tiny little rabbit, I am a little bunny."

"What is the difference?" said the dog.

"Ask any rabbit," said the little bunny.

So the dog sniffed up to a hollow tree and there was a big fat rabbit sitting inside of the tree.

"What is the difference between a rabbit and a little bunny?" said the dog.

"One is little and one is big," said the rabbit, and he shot out of the tree and disappeared over the hill.

So the little dog took a drink of water out of the cold wet stream. When he stuck his nose in the stream he saw little fish that were no longer than an eyelash.

"What little, little tiny fish," said the dog.

"We are not little, little tiny fish," said the fish. "We are minnows."

"What is the difference?" said the dog.

"Ask any fish," said the minnows.

So the little dog reached in the river with a paw and pushed a big fish.

"What is the difference between a minnow and a fish?" asked the dog.

"One is little and one is big," said the fish, and he swam away.

Just then an egg fell out of a nest and broke. Out popped a little duckling with yellow feathers.

"What a funny little duck," said the dog.

"I am not a funny little duck," said the funny little duck. "I am a duckling."

"What is the difference?" said the dog.

"Ask any duck," said the duckling.

So the dog walked along until he met a duck.

"What is the difference between a duck and a duckling?" said the dog.

"One is little and one is big," said the duck, and he waddled away and so did the dog.

He waddled away until he came to a big green field with a fence around it. Inside the fence a very small horse was kicking up his very small heels.

"What a very small horse," said the dog.

"I am not a very small horse," said the very small horse. "I am a young colt."

"What is the difference?" said the dog.

"Ask any horse," said the colt.

So the dog jumped the fence and ran across the field to a big brown horse.

"What is the difference between a horse and a colt?" asked the dog.

"One is little and one is big," said the horse.

68

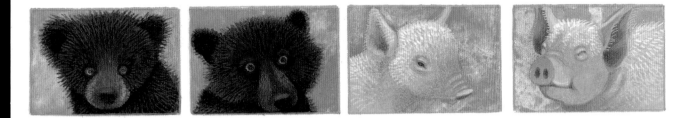

"What's the difference between a cub and a bear?" wondered the dog. "Between a piglet and a pig? A chick and a chicken? A tadpole and a frog?"

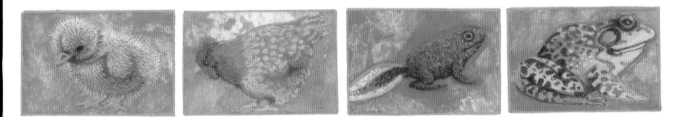

Finally he met a dog.

And the dog said to him, "What a little dog you are."

"No, I am not, I am a little puppy," said the little dog.

"What is the difference between a puppy and a dog?" asked the dog.

"One is little and one is big," said the puppy, for now he understood.

And that was the end of his walk.

Bravery

The Flying Mouse

THERE WAS ONCE A MOUSE who longed for wings, great big wonderful flying things. He wanted to fly away through the sky on great big wings that would carry him high. He wanted to be a flying mouse and fly over everybody's house. He was tired of being a little ground mouse.

And then one time in the middle of the night there came a bright light into his room. And a small voice said, "Little mouse, little mouse, get up and go to the place where the brook flows into the river. And from the second branch of the smallest tree pick two green leaves."

So the little mouse combed his
whiskers and ran down to the place
where the brook flows into the river.
There was a little beech tree that
grew there. And from the second
branch the little mouse picked
two green leaves.

"Now," said the mouse, "I have two
green leaves. But what can a little mouse do with these?"

Then came a bright light again, all over the river. And
a small voice said:

"Little mouse, little
mouse. Take the leaves
you have there. Put them
under your arms and fly
through the air!"

And, lo and behold, the little
mouse took the two green leaves
and flew through the air.

73

And as he flew, the leaves became wings, great big wonderful flying things. And the little mouse began to fly. He flew over the houses of the other mouses.

He flew along with his wings up there. And he flew, and he flew, and he flew through the air. He flew over the treetops and everywhere.

Then he came down out of the air to play with the other mice. But when they saw him, they ran away. They were all afraid and would not play with the flying mouse. Then the little mouse went to tease the cat. And the cat said, "Goodness! What is that?" And electricity flew out of his hair. "I can't chase a mouse up in the air."

The cat switched his tail like a lion in its lair. Whoever saw a mouse flying through the air! He would not play with a flying mouse.

And there in the air, flying everywhere, were terrible bats. They looked like flying rats. Bats!

The bats were glad to see the mouse, and they flew with him into a darkened house.

But the mouse was not very pleased at that. A mouse will never be pleased with a bat. The mouse was not happy there in the dark with the snarling bats, and the hiss and the squeak and the other sounds that bats speak.

When morning came and he looked around, the bats were sleeping upside down. So the little mouse flew down to the ground. He flew to the ground and he ran to the brook. And in the water he took one look!

"Oh, dear me! Now what is that?"

For the flying mouse looked like a little fat bat. And the little mouse did not like that.

Then the little mouse began to shiver, and he ran and he ran and he ran to the river. He sat down under the little beech tree. And he wondered and wondered what on earth he could be.

There was no place on earth for a flying mouse. He didn't want to live in the bat house. And no one would play with a flying mouse.

"Oh, dear me," said the little mouse. "How I wish I were like other mice!"

And, lo and behold, the light came back all over the river. The mouse's wings began to quiver. His wings flew back to be leaves on the tree. And the little mouse danced and cried with glee, "I am ME!"

And the small voice said, "Little mouse, little mouse. Go back to your house and be a mouse!"

One Eye Open

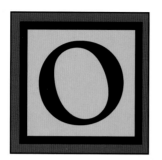NCE THERE WAS A LITTLE CAT who wanted to see the world. So he stuck out his whiskers and went pussyfooting over to tell his mother good-bye. His mother was asleep. But she had one eye open.

"Why do you want to see the world, you funny little kitten?" she said. "Why not just curl up by me and eat and sleep?"

"Because I want to see the world," said the kitten, "and off I go."

"Good-bye," said his mother. "Look where you're going. Look before you leap, and always keep one eye open."

The Tiger's Child

Ssssssssssssspit

I'm Wild Cat Wild

The Tiger's child

I bristle my hairs

And scratch down chairs

And arch my back at terrible bears

I'm Wild Cat Wild

The Tiger's child

Brave Little Airplane

There was once
A brave little airplane
Who flew through the wind
And the snow and the rain
And he heard their songs
Again and again,
The songs that are sung
To an airplane

I am the rain
The rain
The rain
I get you wet
Little Airplane

I am the snow
The snow
The snow
I make you cold
When the cold
    winds blow

I am the wind
The wind
The wind
I blow the snow
I blow the rain
AND I BLOW YOU
Little Airplane

Snow rain wind snow
Will always be
Wherever you go
Rain snow wind rain
Will always be,
Little Airplane.

Love and Friendship

Mouse of My Heart

Mouse mouse

Why do you start

Timid and shy

As a human heart?

Mouse mouse

Where do you glide

Like a soft gray shadow

Trying to hide?

Mouse mouse

Where is your den

Far from the eyes

Of cats and men?

Little Brown Bird

Oh, little brown bird from nowhere
Arriving suddenly through the air
Stay in my garden
Don't go away
And I will watch over
Day after day
Feed you
And cherish your song
And stop
To watch you hop
Among the flowers.

The Lonely Little Colt

HEN DAWN CAME in the barnyard, the little colt was still asleep. His mother nudged him with her nose until she had him on his feet.

The colt shook himself and looked out of the window. But he shook himself too hard. He hadn't been in the world long enough to know how hard a colt should shake himself. His legs were not yet very strong. So down he went on his knees. But soon he was on his feet again and giving stiff little jumps on his brand-new legs. His mother watched him with pride and joy.

He ran with his mother out of the barn and into the fields. Once around the field they galloped. Twice around the field they galloped.

Then the farmer came to the field. He whistled to the mother horse. "It is time for you to go back to work,"

he said. "You have galloped around with your baby long enough. Now you must help me cut a field of clover to make some hay."

Then the farmer took the mother horse away from the field. The little colt was left there all by himself.

At first the little colt wasn't very happy. He had never been left by himself before. And he did not like it. He galloped around close to the fence and neighed for his mother. Then he just galloped around the field faster and faster.

After a while he began to enjoy himself. He felt the warm sunshine. He smelled the green grass. He went to the fence and watched some geese march by. He wished the geese were big enough to play with. But he couldn't gallop around the field with a goose.

Then the brown spotted dog came dashing across the field.

The dog can run with me, thought the little colt. With a kick of his heels, he galloped after the dog.

But the dog would not wait to play that day. He ran right across the field and under the fence where the little colt couldn't go. The brown spotted

90

dog was going to the hill to take care of the sheep. He didn't have time to play with a little colt.

Then the little colt saw a little pig running down the road. He ran over to the fence and neighed to the little pig. But the little pig only squealed and ran away. He was looking for something a little pig could eat. He did not want to play with a little colt.

Then the colt saw a sleepy little calf looking over the fence. The little colt ran over to the calf and stopped. Here was an animal his own size. They rubbed noses.

The little colt kicked up his heels.

Then the little calf kicked up his heels.

The the little colt neighed.

Then the little calf mooed.

The little colt stiffened his legs and jumped.

Then the little calf stiffened his legs and jumped.

After that they seemed to feel that they knew each other. So they ran up and down beside the fence.

The calf ran up and down on his side of the fence.

And the colt ran up and down on his side of the fence.

Then a little boy came and opened the gate, and the colt rushed into the field with the calf. Soon they found another gate open. So they both ran into the farmyard and jumped over everything they saw.

They jumped over a chicken.

They jumped over a cat.

They jumped over a pig,

And they jumped over the bull.

They jumped and they jumped and they jumped.

And then when evening came, the mother horse whinnied and the colt ran home.

And the mother cow mooed and the calf ran home.

All this happened the day the colt and the calf came to know each other. After that, the colt was not lonely anymore.

A Little Black Dog

I had a little black dog

And the sun came out for him

And it shone on his curious little nose

And warmed him warm under his black fur

And he bounded through his sunlight

The sunlight that shone for him.

Bedtime

Two Little Raccoons

Two little raccoons in the moon's dim light
Sat in a tree and held on tight
While a dark bird sang
In the tender night,
"Spoon up the moon
Spoon up the moon
Spoon up the moon."

Drowsy Little Bumblebee

Drowsy little bumblebee

Come and rest your wings on me

No more humming in the sun

Stars come out and day is done.

When I Close My Eyes at Night

When I close my eyes at night

In the darkness I see light

Blue clouds in a big white sky

Where bright green birds go flying by.

The Sleepy Bears

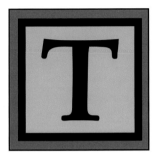HERE WAS A BIG SLEEPY BEAR and a little sleepy bear.

The big sleepy bear yawned a great big yawn, and the little sleepy bear yawned a little sleepy yawn.

Then the big sleepy bear gave a great big stretch, and the little sleepy bear gave a little sleepy stretch.

Then the big sleepy bear got into bed, and the little sleepy man got into bed.

And the big sleepy bear put his head on the pillow, and the little sleepy bear put his head on the pillow.

And the big sleepy bear sang a big sleepy song, and the little sleepy bear sang a little sleepy song.

Then the big sleepy bear told the little sleepy bear a story about the Man in the Moon, who was once a little boy, not much bigger than the little sleepy bear. And about how the little boy Man in the Moon got up every night and ran around all night until by daytime he was so hungry he ate a big fat dinner and stretched and yawned and got into bed and put his head on his pillow, and slowly,

slowly, slowly, and quietly, quietly, quietly, and gently, gently, gently he went day after day after day to sleep and dreamed he was the Man in the Moon.

And the little sleepy bear listened and he never said a word. But he thought about the moonlight, and the starlight and the sunlight at noon, and how he'd be sleeping pretty soon.

Then the big sleepy bear closed his eyes, and the little sleepy bear closed his eyes.

And the little sleepy bear thought of the moon again, and again, and again. And he never said a word because he was sound asleep.

Under the Sun
and the Moon

Go to sleep my bunny

Oh go to sleep my bun

Under the sun and the moon

Go to sleep my bunny

Oh go to sleep my bun

You'll be a big rabbit soon.

Go to sleep my kitty

Oh go to sleep my cat

Under the sun and the moon

Go to sleep my kitty

Oh go to sleep my cat

You'll be a tiger cat soon.

Go to sleep my owlet

Oh go to sleep my owl

Under the sun and the moon

Go to sleep my owlet

Oh go to sleep my owl

And you'll be a hoot owl soon.

103

Go to sleep my puppy

Oh go to sleep my dog

Under the sun and the moon

Go to sleep my puppy

Oh go to sleep my dog

And you'll be a big dog

soon.

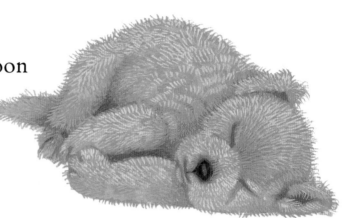

Go to sleep my teddy

Oh go to sleep my bear

Under the sun and the moon

Go to sleep my teddy

Oh go to sleep my bear

And you'll be a big bear soon.

Go to sleep my baby

Oh go to sleep my girl

Under the sun and the moon

Go to sleep my baby

Oh go to sleep my girl

And you'll be a young lady

soon.

Go to sleep my baby

Oh go to sleep my boy

Under the sun and the moon

Go to sleep my baby

Oh go to sleep my boy

And you'll be a grown man

soon.

The Farmer's Lullaby

Silently the first star comes

The moon rides up the sky

The little mice scamper about

    in the hay

And the horses stomp and sigh

One last moo from a dreaming cow

And the old pig winks his eye

And the fireflies blink

through the darkening night

In the farmer's lullaby.

Happiness

The Barnyard Song

The rooster began it
Early in the morning.
Before the sun's dawning,
The rooster began
The Barnyard Song.
"Cock-a-doodle doo!"

Cock-a-
doodle
doo

And the little birds
Carried it along:
"Sweet wheat! Sweet wheat!"

Sweet
wheat

Sweet
wheat

"Cluck, cluck, cluck!"

The chickens chimed in, too.

Cluck

Cluck

Cluck

"Baa," sang the little lambs.

Baa

"Oink," sang the pig,

"I'll sing 'Ugh, ugh, ugh,'

When I get big."

Oink

109

Where Is the Spring?

"On a bush," sang the robin

"In the sky," sang the lark.

In a song

In the spring

In the dark.

Red Cherries

Up in a cherry tree in the sun
The cherries ripened one by one
Big red cherries, there they hung
And I ate them in the sun.

Some were yellow, some were red
And birds were singing round my head.
On their slender stems they hung
And I ate them one by one.

Spring was late, I couldn't wait.

O Pussywillows

A small gray kitten
Went walking in spring.
On a moonlit night
You could hear him sing.
To pussywillows
He would sing and purr
Because like kittens
They have soft gray fur.

"O pussywillows,"
The kitten would sing
"Gray pussywillows
First sign of spring

You come in the woods
All furry and warm
You bloom in the woods
Then—pouf—you are gone."

"O pussywillows,"
The kitten would purr
"Gray little flowers
All covered in fur
Today you are here
And now you are near
All of a sudden
Must you disappear?"

Spring Still Spring

The fern uncurls in the wet spring woods

And the trillium blooms

And the first bee booms

Around and around

Where a rabbit nips the new garden leaves

As they spring up in the spring.

Belonging

I Dreamed of a Horse

I dreamed of a horse

A quiet horse

And the horse belonged to me

I dreamed of a horse

A great white horse

In a land beyond the sea

I dreamed of a horse

A golden horse

In the time of chivalry

I dreamed of a horse

A gentle horse

And the horse belonged to me.

Three Baby Kittens

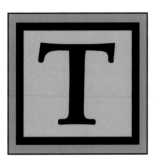THREE BABY KITTENS were once born into this world.

One was black. One was white. One was a calico kitten.

And when they felt the warmth of their own little bodies, they all began to purr, for they thought the world was wonderful.

They even thought that the mean old farmer who owned them was wonderful. And just as soon as they could crawl, they crawled all over his house. But the farmer did not like kittens.

"One cat on a farm is enough," the mean old farmer said to his son. "We do not have room for three kittens, too."

"I know what to do," the farmer's son said. He put the three kittens in an old gunnysack. "These three little kittens will find a home if I take them into town."

The gunnysack was wonderful, too. They rolled about in the cozy darkness of the sack and wrestled and hugged each other. Then they curled up in a warm pile of fur and went to sleep.

The farmer's son hit a bump in the road.

The old gunnysack flew up into the air. It came down in a soft bank of snow.

The kittens blinked open their eyes and yawned. One by one they crawled out of the old gunnysack.

They did not see the farmer's son driving away.

They did not know they were all alone.

All they knew was that the white snow was wonderful. They went creeping across it. Their bright little kitten eyes were shining like stars in the night. The snow began to fall softly in the empty garden. The little black kitten batted it with his paw. And the other two kittens went pouncing after the soft snowflakes as they drifted toward the ground.

It was the little black kitten that found the cellar window open.

With long leaps through the snow, the other two kittens followed him in through the open window. First they came into exciting black darkness.

The little black kitten blinked his bright yellow eyes in the darkness. The little white kitten blinked two little green eyes, and the little calico kitten blinked her great big yellow eyes. For kittens can see in the dark.

The three baby kittens crept ahead until they came to some steps. The steps were steep and hard to climb. But, one by one, each little kitten pulled itself up—step by step. At the top of the steps was a long crack of light. Beyond was a kitchen full of good cooking smells.

Three little kitten heads came peeking through the door. And there was the most wonderful thing of all: milk! There was a full saucer of it, warm from the warmth of the room. The little kittens drank it so fast, they spattered it all over their faces.

They were sitting under a stove, licking each other.

They were clean and dry when they heard the big feet coming. They were big feet, the biggest feet the kittens had ever seen. The feet came nearer. Two hands put a pie on the kitchen table. Then the feet went away.

It didn't take the three kittens long to climb right up on the table and sniff around the pie. Then the little black kitten pounced right into the middle of the pie and squirted the red juice of it into the white kitten's eye. The little calico kitten just stood on the other side of the pie and waited, with her eyes shining. And when the little black kitten crawled out of the pie and onto the table, they grabbed him. They grabbed the black kitten and gave him a good cat-scrubbing with their tongues.

Then the little black kitten went pouncing too near the edge of the tablecloth and fell. Down, down he went, pulling the whole tablecloth with him. Plates and pans came crashing down. The little white kitten slid down the tablecloth like a shoot-the-chute.

And the pie landed right on top of him. The kittens liked the noise of the crash. It was such a big, exciting noise. Then they licked themselves clean once more and went off to explore the rest of the house.

In the dining room, they saw a feather blowing about in the air. The black kitten began a dance with it. He jumped into the air and smacked the feather with his paw. The calico kitten danced, too. But it was the white kitten that discovered the hot air coming up through the grate in the floor. He put

his paw in it. But the air blew right past him. He couldn't see what it was, but he knew that it was warm and soft and wonderful. He waved his paw in it back and forth, back and forth.

Then they discovered the piano. *Ping pang! Ping pang!*—kittens on the keys. The black kitten danced on the high notes, and the white kitten danced on the low notes.

At that, in came the two big feet. And the two big feet chased the three baby kittens all over the house.

Finally, the kittens ran upstairs and hid in the little girl's room. They hid in her closet, and each little kitten climbed into a shoe and went to sleep.

The little black kitten climbed into a soft red slipper and went to sleep.

124

The other two kittens climbed into a pair of sneakers and went to sleep.

There they were when the little girl found them. They were all curled up in her shoes—three sleepy baby soft angel kittens. And the little girl loved them and kept them forever. And the kittens thought the little girl was wonderful.

Even the cook, who owned the big feet, grew to love the three baby kittens.

The Ugly Duckling

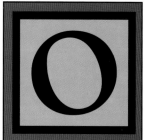NCE UPON A TIME there were two ducks. They had their nest on the edge of a pond in a far corner of the world.

In the nest were five round, smooth eggs.

When the mother duck wasn't sitting on the nest, the father duck was sitting on the nest. All the time they were waiting for some little ducklings to come out of the eggs.

They waited for a long time. The father duck walked up and down. He walked up and down so much that he wore a deep path in the earth where he walked.

And then one day there came a *pick-pick-pick* from inside the eggs. And, one by one, out tumbled four tiny yellow ducklings. When they came tumbling over the edge of the nest, the father duck looked at them with pride and joy.

Then there came a *pick-pick-pick* from inside the fifth egg. Out tumbled the fifth duckling!

There he stood on one foot. He did not look like the others. His feathers were white instead of yellow. His neck was longer. His eyes were big and staring.

When the other ducklings saw him, they ran and hid under their mother's wing. The mother duck stood there and looked. Never had she hatched a duck like this before.

The father duck came running over with a quack-quack-quack.

"Where did this thing come from?" he asked.

"You must have laid that egg," said the mother duck.

"I don't lay eggs!" said the father duck. "Quack! Quack! Quack! Where did this little thing come from?"

The little thing stood there with a piece of eggshell on his head like a hat. He looked around him for the first time. He was so very happy to be born. He looked at the tall green grasses and the pink water lilies of the brand-new world he was living in. He did not know he was an ugly duckling.

Then the mother duck took her little ducklings for their first walk. She shooed the yellow ducklings on ahead of her. The ugly duckling came waddling along behind. But when he tried to come close to the mother duck, she shooed him away.

"You're no child of mine," she seemed to say. Still, the ugly duckling tagged along.

When the ducklings went for their first swim, the ugly duckling paddled his legs under him right along with the others.

"Well!" said the mother duck. "At least he's a swimming bird. But he certainly is a funny duck. Come, little ducklings, climb onto my back."

The little ducklings climbed onto her back with a quack-quack-quack.

The ugly duckling swam very fast and climbed on, too. Then he made his first noise.

"Honk! Honk!" he said.

What a strange noise for a duckling!

The mother duck and the little ducklings ducked their heads. Who ever heard of a honking duck! They pushed the ugly duckling off the mother duck's back and into the water. A duck who honked did not belong to them.

Then the mother duck and her ducklings swam off and left the little ugly duckling diving around by himself. He was very lonesome.

He only looked back once at the yellow-feathered backs of the other ducklings as they swam after their mother. Then he went away all by himself.

The poor little duckling swam and swam until he was very tired. Then he climbed up onto the dry land.

Standing there, he looked down into the dark blue water. There in the water was his reflection, all twisted by the ripples of the stream. He did not look like the other ducklings. His eyes were too big, and his neck was too long. His feathers were white instead of yellow.

And then he knew he was an ugly duckling. Big tears came out of his eyes and fell on the ground.

Poor little duckling! Another big tear squeezed out of one eye.

He was not wanted. He was an ugly duckling, and nobody loved him. So he wandered off all alone through the marshes—one little duck in the wide, wide world.

As he walked along, he did not see that the rushes grew green by the bank, and red-winged blackbirds were singing in the sunlight.

Suddenly he heard chirping. Looking up, he saw four friendly little marsh birds chirping to him from a nest in a fallen tree.

The ugly duckling gave a little honk and climbed right up into the nest with them. The baby birds chirped lovingly around him. The nest was warm and the little birds were soft beside him.

All at once the little birds opened up their bills, and along came flying the old marsh bird who was their mother. She had a big worm which she threw to them for their supper.

But when the ugly duckling caught it, the mother bird squawked with rage and pulled the worm away.

She chased the duckling from her nest, pecked him on the head, and beat him with her wings.

The little duckling ran and ran until he jumped into the water. Then he swam away as fast as he could. He swam so fast that he bumped right smack into a wooden duck and started it rocking.

When the ugly duckling saw the big wooden duck, he rubbed his little head against the duck's wooden breast. He didn't know that it was just a wooden duck painted in wild-bird colors. He didn't know that the wooden duck was put there by hunters to lure real wild ducks! He simply thought, Here is a friend.

The wooden duck did not swim away from him. Instead it let the ugly duckling climb up onto the end of its tail and bounce up and down there.

He was so happy that he gave a big bounce in the air that landed him in water. This tipped the wooden duck so far forward that when it rocked back again, it smacked the little duckling on the head.

The ugly duckling thought his new friend had knocked into him on purpose, so he swam off down the stream, the saddest little duck in the world.

He hid in the reeds that grew along the riverbank and honked as though his little heart would break. His tears fell into the water and made little circles there. He stopped to watch one tear hit the water. Then he put his head down on the ground and cried and cried.

Just then a great white mother swan and her four little swans came floating down the river.

They stopped and listened when they heard the little duck honking on the shore. And when the little swans saw the ugly duckling with his head down on the ground, they came swimming over to him.

"Honk! Honk! Honk!" the swans called to him.

When he heard the sound, the

ugly duckling looked around and saw the four baby swans. They were as white as he was, and they all had long necks like his own. They were honking to him in a friendly way. He was so happy he dove right into his own reflection in the water and broke it. When he came up, the little swans were still there.

The young swans played with him and swam in circles around him.

Then the great white mother swan honked to the little swans. The ugly duckling looked up and saw her. Never had he seen such a beautiful white curving bird. The baby swans all went swimming back to the great white swan.

The little duckling watched them go. He wished he might grow up to be beautiful like these swans. Then he remembered he was an ugly duckling. His little head dropped, and he started to swim off by himself, all alone on the wide waters of the stream.

But the swans would not let him go. They knew that the ugly duckling was really a baby swan, just like them. So the white swans swam around the little lost swan and stroked his neck with their beaks. The mother let him come near to the soft swan's down on her breast.

Then she put her wing over her lost baby swan and swam with him down the stream.

The Grasshopper
and the Ants

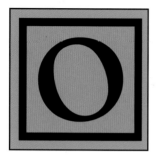"*Oh, the world owes me a living,*

Tra la la, lalala la."

The grasshopper was singing his song as he jumped through his fields.

He almost jumped on top of some ants who were pulling grains of corn up an anthill.

Said the grasshopper to the ants: "Why are you working all through the day? A summer day is a time to play!"

"We can't," said the ants. "Winter will soon be here."

The busy little ants did not have time to feel the warm summer sun or to run and jump just for fun. From the beginning of day till the end, they were busy hauling the corn away. Winter was coming. They had no time to play.

All summer the grasshopper sang and danced his grasshopper dances in the grasses. When he was hungry, he reached out and ate.

And the grasshopper sang:

"The good book says: 'The world provides.
There's food on every tree.'
Why should anyone have to work? Not me!
Oh, the world owes me a living, tra la la, lalala la."

With that, he took a big swig of honey from a blue harebell that grew above his head. Then he spit a big wet spit of grasshopper tobacco juice. It nearly landed on a little ant who was dragging a load of cherries to store in the ant house for the winter.

Said the grasshopper to the ant:

"The other ants can work all day.
Why not try the grasshopper's way?
Come on, let's sing and dance and play!
Oh, the world owes me a living, tra la la, lalala la."

The little ant was so charmed by the music that he dropped his heavy load and started to dance.

Then came the queen, the Queen of All the Ants.

And the Queen of All the Ants frowned on the dancing ant so that he picked up his cherries and went back to the other busy ants. The Queen of All the Ants spoke sober words to the grasshopper: "You'll change your tune when winter comes and the ground is white with snow."

But the grasshopper only made a courtly bow.

141

"Winter is a long way off," he said. "Do you dance? Let's go."

Oh, the world owes me a living, tra la la, lalala la.
The other ants can work all day.
Why not try the grasshopper's way?
Come on, let's sing and dance and play!

But even as he sang and played on his fiddle, the Queen of All the Ants hurried away. She, like other ants, had no time to play.

All through the long, lazy summer months the grasshopper went on singing:

Oh, the world owes me a living, tra la la, lalala la.

There was no tomorrow. There was only today, and the sleet and snow seemed far away. But the little ants worked harder than ever. As long as the sun was in the sky, they went back and forth carrying the foods from the fields into their ant house.

Then the winter wind began to blow. It blew the leaves off all the trees. The ants ran into their ant house and closed the door, and you didn't see them in the fields anymore. Every day the winds would blow. And then one day—SNOW.

The grasshopper was freezing. He couldn't find any leaves to eat. All he had was his fiddle and his bow. And he wandered along, lost in the snow. He had nothing to eat and nowhere to go. Then far off he saw one leaf still clinging to a tree.

"Food! Food!" cried the hungry grasshopper, and he leaned against the wind and pushed on toward the tree.

But just as he got there, the wind blew the last dry leaf

away. The grasshopper dropped his fiddle and watched the leaf go. It fluttered away through the white snowflakes. It drifted slowly away. It was gone.

And then he came to the house of the busy ants. He could hear them inside having a dance. They had worked hard all summer, and now they could enjoy the winter.

The grasshopper was too cold to go on. The wind blew him over, and he lay where he fell. His long green jumping and dancing legs were nearly frozen. Then, very slowly, he pulled himself to the house of the ants and knocked.

When the ants came to the door, they found him there, half frozen. And ten of the kind and busy ants came out and carried the poor grasshopper into their house. They gave him hot corn soup. And they hurried about, making him warm.

Then the Queen of All the Ants came to him. And the grasshopper was afraid, and he begged of her: "Oh, Madam Queen, wisest of ants, please, please, give me another chance."

The Queen of All the Ants looked at the poor, thin frozen grasshopper as he lay shivering there. Then she spoke these words:

"With ants, just those that work may stay. So take your fiddle—and PLAY!"

145

The grasshopper was so happy that his foot began beating out the time in the old way, and he took up his fiddle and sang:

"I owe the world a living, tra la la, lalala la.
I've been a fool the whole year long.
Now I'm singing a different song.
You were right, I was wrong. Tra la la, lalala la."

Then all of the ants began to dance, even the Queen of All the Ants.

And the grasshopper sang:

"Now I'm singing a different song.
I owe the world a living, tra la la, lalala la."

For a
Rainy Day

The Hollow Tree

Oh, happy, happy, hollow tree

Where the bear and the bug and the grub
 and the bee

Sleep all winter drowsily

In their warm dark honeycombed tree

Drowsily sleep in their dark and hollow tree.

Raindrops on the Willow Tree

The diamonds on the tree twigs

Are all the diamonds that I've got

So bright

So unexpected

So soon gone

And yet

Alive as rain

Alive as time

Shining like diamonds

Raindrops

They shine and glow

Brighter than snow

They shine

And they are mine.

Smoky Nights

Smoky nights

And the half-lit lights

Of streetlights

In the smoky night

Of October evening

Of lighted doors

That open

Into home.

Quiet Rain

O the beautiful rain is wet is wet

And yet I cannot forget forget

The sound of the train in the distant rain

And the sound of the rain dripping down

So light, so light, so white, so light

Quieter quieter grows the night

The rain has turned to snow.

The Old Mill

A S THE SUN LEFT THE SKY, the clouds in the west were gold and gray. The peace of evening came down over the land.

The spider hurried to weave the last strands of his web before dark. The cows went slowly home across the ridge of the hill. And the ducks waddled into the barn.

The windmill stood with its giant ragged arms against the evening sky. Quietness came all around.

The blue barn swallow with the red throat swooped into the old mill. He carried a worm in his beak for his little mate, who was keeping warm their three blue eggs. They were at home in the old mill. Their nest was made in a cog hole of the millstone, for the old mill had not been used for many years except as a home for birds and other animals. As darkness came on, the old fat owl who slept

through the day opened his round yellow eyes. He cocked his head and stamped from one foot to the other. Then he called in a sleepy way, "Whoo! Whoo! Whoo!"

Farther up, bright eyes came out like electric lights in the darkness under the roof. These were the eyes of the bats.

The bats lived in the old mill, too, hanging upside down as they slept through the day.

One bat after another unfolded its wings and stretched them wide. They fluttered forth from the old mill like ragged scattered leaves.

Outside, the moon came up in a soft golden mist. The crickets began to chirp in the summer night.

On the pond, as the last of the water lilies closed, two big eyes peered from under a lily pad.

Out jumped a big green bullfrog.

He jumped on a lily pad and croaked:

"Come! Come! Come! Come!"

And another frog croaked:

"Come where! Come where!

Come! Come! Come where!

Come! Come!"

Another frog answered:

"Come here! Come where! Come! Come!"

A great chorus of frogs was croaking on the lily pads of the pond. Lightning bugs made hundreds of golden sparks in the darkness.

Then the wind began to blow. It swept through the trees. Great black clouds sailed over the moon. The wind blew harder. Leaves fell down from the trees into the pond, and the frogs dived under the water. *Plop!*

Then the storm came on in all of its crashing fury.

The old fat owl, sitting on a rafter above the mill's waterwheel, was nearly thrown from his perch. Water dripped on the fat owl's head and made him angry. He seemed to grow bigger and bigger as he ruffled up his feathers in anger.

Outside, the wind blew the trees low and blew down the fence posts. The slender reeds in the swamp broke off at their lower joints.

Then, in the fury of the storm, the rope that held the mill wheel broke! The arms of the old mill were free once more. They turned round and round against the sky, and the big wheel inside the mill began to turn.

The mother bird on her nest saw the great wheel coming down above her. She fluttered away from the nest in fright. But then she flew back and covered her wings. She did not know that the cog for that hole in the millstone was broken. And so the big wheel came rolling over her nest and left her unhurt.

Around and around, the great jagged arms of the windmill turned against the sky. Black clouds went racing over the moon. Lightning flashed in jagged cracks.

And inside the mill the great wheel turned around and around over the little mother barn swallow.

The wind shrieked outside, but the little swallow never left her nest.

157

She covered it and kept the eggs warm.

Lightning flashed close by the fat old owl, so he moved sideways on his perch. Then he blinked and turned his head.

The lightning came again with a deafening crash. It struck the old mill and broke off one of the arms of the windmill. The old mill shook, and its turning wheel went more slowly.

The wind died down, and there was only the sound of the rain. And the sound of the rain grew softer and softer until it went away. Then the sky outside grew yellow and light in the east. The moon was gone. And the old mill stood as before. Only now one ragged arm was broken and hanging down against the morning sky.

Inside the mill the old fat owl blinked and closed his eyes. And the bats came flying home. In the nest under the mill wheel three little birds were opening yellow bills. And the mother and father swallow came flying in. They had worms

for their baby birds, who had been born during the storm. The blue feathers of the baby barn swallows were shining in the morning sun.

All was peaceful, as though the storm had never been. The cows went slowly over the hill. The ducks came out of the barn and swam back to the green reeds by the edge of the pond.

All was quiet as before. The storm had come and gone. And the sunlight was caught in the spider's web.

Nonsense

Nonsense Song

A long way from Nowhere

In the Land of Nothing

Two pussycats sat in a tree.

How did they get there?

And where did they come from?

On that they could never agree.

Whoopsie Daisy!

Whoopsie Daisy
Picked a daisy
On a summer's day.
Whoopsie Daisy
Picked a daisy
Then she ran away!

Snowballs and Sunshine

Summer summer in the sun

Flowers grow and bunnies run

And it's always the same little boy

And it's always the same little girl

Snowballs snowballs in the snow

Snowflakes fall

and cold winds blow

Pussywillows in the spring

Violets bloom and robins sing

166

The winds blow hard
across the hill
And slap the yellow daffodil

Grasshoppers, ladybugs, and bees
Hop about bare toes and knees

The fog comes on without

  a sound

Gray—silent—all around

Rain rain on the windowpane

Splashes once then splashes again

Walk across the icy snow

No footsteps wherever you go

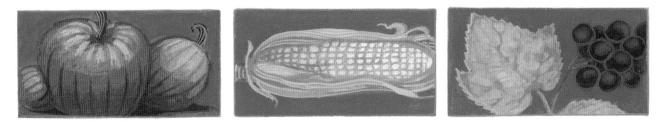

Orange pumpkins yellow corn

Purple grapes and frosty morn

The smoke is drifting all around

From raked leaves on the ground

Jagged lightning splits the sky

Thunder rumbles,

wild winds cry

Starlight starlight frosty bright

In the spaces of the night

Colors

Apple Trees

Apple trees as pink as pie

Like strawberry ice cream

In the sky

Burst on my

Delighted eye.

Golden Air

When the wind blows
The leaves fall free
Yellow leaves falling
In golden air

And everywhere
Upon the ground
Leaves of gold
Are scattered round.

All the Bright Colors

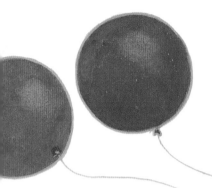

Happy happy colors
Colors of carrots and peas

Red the color of
red balloons

Green of grasses
and trees

Gray the color
of winter skies

Purple of tropical seas

Blue the color of
Concord grapes

Yellow the
stripes of bees

Happy happy colors
Color of autumn leaves.

Nature

One Night

The moon came out of the sea one night
Into a dark blue sky.
It made an enormous yellow light
Across the dark night sky.

The stars came out of the sea one night
And went up across the sky.
They came with a clear and still light
High in the dark blue sky.
They seemed to be not far away
And not so very high.

The Life of a Leaf

In the spring

The leaf began as a bud

Then fell to the ground with a thud

In the fall of the year.

The summer is brief

And so is the life of a leaf.

Dream of a Weed

Dream of a weed growing from a seed

Quietly, quietly from a seed

In a garden

A slim green weed

Quietly, quietly from a seed.

Clouds

A cloud is a cloud

A great big soft white wonderful thing

In an even bigger sky

And sometimes not so high

But near enough to fly

Up there and lie

In the softness of that

Cloud in the sky

And sink till you no longer think

But only drift

And in that drift through endless blue

A soft white cloud is lifting you

Through the softer air.

Index

Index

All the Little Fathers *61*
All the Bright Colors *174*
Animals in the Snow *28*
Apple Trees *172*

Baby Hippopotamus *53*
Barnyard Song, The *108*
Brave Little Airplane *81*
Bug's Poem, A *55*

Clouds *180*
Cottontail Rabbit in a
    Cotton Field, A *6*

Diggers, The *40*
Dream of a Weed *179*
Drowsy Little
    Bumblebee *97*

Farmer's Lullaby, The *106*
Flying Mouse, The *72*
Four Fur Feet *25*
From a Hornet's Nest *27*

Glorious Flight of the
    Mouse, The *10*
Golden Air *173*
Grasshopper and the Ants,
    The *138*

Index

Hollow Tree, The 148

I Dreamed of a Horse 116

Life of a Leaf, The 178
Little Black Dog, A 94
Little Brown Bird 86
Little Pig's Picnic, The 15
Lonely Little Colt, The 87

Mouse of My
    Heart 84

Nonsense Song
   162

O Pussywillows 112
Old Mill, The 152
One Eye Open 78
One Night 176
Quiet Rain 151

Raindrops on the
    Willow Tree 149

Red Cherries 111
Run, Bun, Run 8

Said a Bug 56
Sleepy Bears, The 99

Smoky Nights *150*

Snowballs and Sunshine *165*

Song of Little Things *54*

"Spring!" Sang the Bird *39*

Spring Still Spring *114*

Three Baby Kittens *117*

Three Snowmen, The *59*

Three White Rabbits Running *9*

Tiger's Child, The *80*

Two Little Raccoons *96*

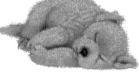

Ugly Duckling, The *126*

Under the Sun and the Moon *102*

What a Little Man *64*

When I Close My Eyes at Night *98*

Where Is the Spring? *110*

Whoopsie Daisy! *164*

You Be Little and I'll Be Big *48*